The Christmas Snowlights

The Christmas Snowlights

Eleanore Tashenberg

To order additional copies of this book, contact:
Xlibris Corporation
1-888-795-4274
www.Xlibris.com
Orders@Xlibris.com
128758

In loving memory and regard
to my dad, Stanley A. Sojka,
a creative storyteller,
and
to his grandson, Brad, Jr.,
who loved his stories

It was a pink morning. A brushstroke of yellow orange painted its way from the sun down the mountains to the snow-covered plains below. It was a day that Marcy enjoyed.

As Marcy fluttered the sleep off her feathers, she thought, *I think I'll look for Pud today.*

So she primped and fluffed her feathers with her beak. She rearranged the straw and grass in her nest. Marcy gave one more shake of her head and flew up to meet the crisp dawn of the wintry day.

Marcy flew over the small town of Bethlehem. It was not far from her nest.

Pud was a peculiar critter. He was also very particular.

"Toooo many people . . . toooo many people," Pud muttered to himself, as he paced back and forth in front of his burrow.

"Donkeys, carts, soldiers, shepherds, carpenters, tent makers, cats, dogs, roosters, sheep," he listed. "Is all of Israel moving to Bethlehem?"

As he sat on a stone just outside his hole, he quietly thought, *No peace . . . no peace!* As he continued thinking, the sound of his name got in the way.

"PUD! PUD! Up here. It's me, Marcy."

Startled, Pud slid off the stone, doing a backward flip, and landed with a squish in the morning snow.

"O-hhh, my whiskers! Oh, my snout, my poor, poor snout. They will be cold for hours. They might wrinkle," Pud moaned.

Marcy landed like a fluff next to Pud. She stretched out her brown wing to help Pud up.

He was always easy to help. Pud was a small creature—a *very very* small critter. Pud was a pika! The tiniest rabbit that God ever made.

How Marcy loved her friend! Pud was the only creature in Bethlehem who would listen to her meadowlark songs. Their friendship was special.

Pud complained a lot!

Marcy sang a lot!

They shared their friendship a lot!

Bethlehem had so much room and they had so much room for each other. These two saw each other through simple eyes, for they were tender-hearted, one to another.

"Let me warm your snout and dry your whiskers," said Marcy, caringly. Pud lifted his face and placed it in Marcy's wings.

Their friendship also talked a lot! "Do you know the news out of Jerusalem?" Marcy asked.

"A lot of dust," joked Pud, in a muffled voice.

"They call this traveling a census," said Marcy.

"I call it a crow-w-wding," Pud answered with annoyance.

Marcy continued, "The soldiers say that the city of Rome wants to count us. Seems that Rome wants to know how many people are alive."

"Too many," sniffed Pud, shivering just a bit.

Marcy gently moved a little closer to Pud to warm him. Pud didn't notice.

"Pud," Marcy whispered, "the sun is higher now and warmer. Let's go to the shepherd's field and find your favorite rock. I can sing a new song while you warm yourself, sunning on the rock. We can do peace!"

When Pud heard this, he livened up and ran off shouting, "Let's goooo . . . Marcy."

What a joyful sight to see the wonder of friendship playfully making tracks in the fresh morning snow and to hear its sound in the song of the meadowlark.

Pikas enjoy sun-bathing, and Pud was no different. No sooner had the two found the rock than Pud scampered and hopped on the smallest stone; then, the next bigger one, like stairs, till he reached his favorite spot—the flat of the big rock.

Pud rolled on his back, paws up and found sleep.

Marcy perched nearby and watched the road that leads to Jerusalem. Normally quiet, this morning it was very busy with the comings and goings as the census required. For, to be counted, people had to return to their birthplace.

How odd humans are, thought Marcy, *demanding such grand activity just to count themselves!* She paused.

"I am one meadowlark!" She paused. "That wasn't difficult." She paused. "I didn't have to move to do it." She paused. This time longer. "Times seem changeable!"

Feeling confident in her newly found wisdom, she hopped about the rocky area till she found a grassy perch and nestled in it.

Keeping one eye on Pud, who now was fully asleep in the warming sun, she lowered her head close to her chest. Puffing her feathers, Marcy settled into her usual routine-watching over Pud and dreaming songs.

Signs and wonders.
Wonders and signs
The words of the prophets
Point to these times.
The heavens awakened.
Uncertain are men.
The peace of the promise
Lost and forgotten.

The day turned gentle. A cool wind stirred and wrapped itself around a warm stream of sunlight and soothed the two friends in rest. Cuddled and comfortable, the two left the busy day for a peaceful nap.

Slowly, sunset and night walked the road to Bethlehem!

"WATCH! LOOK OUT! BE CAREFUL! NO! NO-OO—"

Marcy woke to the alarm. It was Pud. Flying swiftly toward Pud, the problem was obvious.

In the half-black color of evening, Marcy saw a man beginning to step on the very rock where Pud had been roused from sun-sleeping.

The man's first step had caught Pud's whiskers. At a time like this, being very little is a good quality. For Pud quickly hopped-hopped off the rock, just avoiding the sandal of the second step.

"Pud, that was close," said Marcy, as she landed quietly next to Pud.

"My snout . . . my whiskers. They are ruined!" Pud was irritated but scared. Both huddled at the base of the rock and tried to see what was going to happen next.

"Mary, what is wrong?"

"Joseph, the baby is coming."

Using the rock as a step, the man helped the woman off the back of the donkey. He removed his cloak and spread it on the rock.

"Sit on this rock for a while, Mary. Rest. Bethlehem is not far." Pointing down the road, the man comforted the woman.

"See the light. There is an inn."

As the last warm rays of the sun were tucked behind the hills, the night chill gripped.

"Joseph. I am cold. I must make ready for the baby." Her warm and gentle voice broke through the chill of the evening.

"Then we will press on." Taking her hands, the man helped the woman up and then eased her on the back of the donkey.

"God is with us this night, Mary," said the man, as he fixed his cloak over the woman to keep her warm.

"Be of courage, for the journey is near end."

As the man led the donkey away, Marcy and Pud peered around the edge of the rock and watched this tiny caravan disappear down the road.

"What light? What baby? What about my poor snout? Hmm?" Pud asked less scared but still irritated.

"Quiet, Pud. Listen."

"What is it?"

"Listen!"

"Listen, to what?" Pud whispered in his kind of manner.

"There is a stillness. Something reverent has come. Feel the peace? A change is coming, Pud . . . A change . . . ."

"I know! CROWDS!" Pud smirked.

"Let's follow the man and the woman," encouraged Marcy.

"I know the innkeeper," Pud offered, "and 1 heard that there is no place to stay in all of Bethlehem. What will they do? . . . And what is this light that they saw?" asked Pud.

Marcy didn't know. So the two friends headed toward Bethlehem—toward the inn. A sense of wonder began to fill the night.

Puffs of snowflakes slowly began falling to dust the clear silent night. Pud, hopping his very best hop toward the inn, didn't notice the new snowfall. But, Marcy had to keep fluttering her wings to keep them clear so she could still fly.

". . . no room."

As Pud and Marcy came to the inn, they could hear voices.

". . . no room! . . . no room!"

"But, kind sir," said the man called Joseph, "a child is to be born this night. My wife must have a place to lie."

The innkeeper complained, "I have NO room! Bethlehem is overcrowded. Food is scarce. 1 have no . . . 1 have no . . . 1 have . . ." The innkeeper paused in his sentence, then continued with relieved reply. "I HAVE A STABLE. That's it. Around back. You can stay there."

Placing his hand on the innkeeper's shoulder, Joseph spoke a grateful "Thank you, sir. God bless your kindness." With a loving touch, Joseph squeezed Mary's hand and led the donkey to the stable.

As Pud and Marcy followed the weary travelers, Marcy sighed, "It is a place, but it is a cold night. What of the babe?"

Pud knew his way around the stable. He hopped his way to the loft, which was rich with hay. Marcy landed next to him. They watched. They listened. It was dark.

"Joseph, we will need a place to lay the baby. One that is warm and safe. Cloth, too, to wrap the child for warmth."

A soft glow began to lighten a dark corner. The man had lit a small oil lamp. In that dim orange glow, a tiny bundle of life moved in the woman's arms and the baby cried—a *boy*.

Pud acted. Turning around on a hop, he began shoving hay from the loft into the manger below. Marcy had never seen Pud so full of work.

Then it happened. A beam of light came through a crack in the stable's roof. It covered Pud. It spread and stretched till it settled over the manger, which now was overflowing with hay. Pud didn't notice.

Joseph came to the manger, looked up toward the light, and then began arranging the hay. The man and woman talked to each other. A sound of joy was growing in the stable. The woman laughed. The man began a low song.

Pud nudged Marcy with his snout and said, "We are not finished! Fly, quickly, Marcy, where the posts meet the roof. I've hidden strips of cloth there. Get them. Give them to the woman to wrap her baby. I'll get the rest."

Marcy flew up and began tugging and pulling at the cloth. Bringing one at a time, she flew and dropped them before the woman. Then Mary wrapped her baby in these swaddling clothes.

Pud had just gotten the largest cloth into the manger when Mary lay the babe into it. Pud rounded his red, furry body into a ball and waited to be bumped. He wasn't brushed away! He slowly raised his head. His big, round eyes looked into the eyes of the child. At that moment, Pud knew he was part of the wonder of that night.

It was at the same moment that Pud noticed the light. The light seemed warm and safe. Cautiously, Pud's eyes followed the stream of light upward.

"The STAR! This is what Marcy once sang about—the guiding light!"

Humbled by a simple heart, Pud spotted a sprig of rosemary caught in the hay. He took the rosemary and lovingly placed it just above the head of the sleeping babe.

For remembrance! Pud thought.

Then a voice, seemingly outside and within Pud said,

This is the Promise.
This is my Peace.
This is my Love.

Pud's round ears twitted and his nose wiggled. His heart burst with joy as he exclaimed: "E.E. Emmanuel? . . . Em . . . Manuel? . . . EMMANUEL!!!!!"

Then, with a Pud-like thought, he mumbled, "But you're so tiny—so little—like me!" He wiggled a pleased grin.

Marcy's excitement had taken her up to the roof. From there she could see an amber glow from the shepherd's field. Curious, she flew to see what was happening. As she flew towards the field, she happened to look back at the stable. To her surprise, the simple light began to grow brighter and brighter and brighter till it filled the entire stable.

Wonder of wonders! thought Marcy.
"I know this light. The wise of the old days told of a great light that once filled the temple. They called it the Glory of God."

Swallowing on an epiphany, she realized: "God is with us! The Glory has returned! It has a new home—a new Temple! Rejoice in the . . ."

Phump! Bumph!

Before Marcy could finish her thought, she crashed into something in the air.

"ALLELUIA! ALLELUIA!"

Those words came as a blast from a trumpet and sent her tumbling smack into a soft cloud. No! It was the hair of an angel. Her beak got tangled in the hair, and her claw was snagged on the halo.

Marcy pulled hard, only to have "GLORY TO GOD IN THE HIGHEST!" send her spinning into an angel's wing. THUMPH!

Marcy tried to get her flight back on course, but the multitude of heavenly hosts made that quite difficult.

Like riding the waves of a stormy sea, Marcy rose on the swells of alleluias and crashed with the glorias. In a joyous and exalted sea of rejoicing in God, Marcy seemed to rise higher and higher through the heavenly chorus.

Suddenly, Marcy found herself suspended above the highest notes of the music, looking down at the angels and the shepherds and the newly fallen snow.

"Oh-o! I've never been this high," Marcy noted sternly, trying not to be afraid. She was so close to the stars!

"I don't think Rome could count all these," quipped Marcy, still trying to be unafraid.

"My wings are not flapping. What's holding me up?" Now she was frightened.

Then a voice, seemingly outside and from within Marcy, spoke: "Precious songbird. Do not be afraid. I am watching over you."

"How?" asked Marcy, simply.

"I hold you in the palm of my hand."

Marcy's meadowlark spirit felt that she was now in the presence of the Holy Creator—the Giver of life.

Marcy felt awkward and fumbled for a thought or a song or something.

"THANK YOU!" her heart blurted, for her heart was full of rejoicing.

"You kept your promise." Marcy spoke. nervously as she laid one wing over her face, trying to hide her smallness.

"You took a long time though," asserted Marcy, shifting a bit nervously on her claws.

"Just in the blink of an eye!"

"Well, it seemed longer," said Marcy.

"Songbird, sing for me."

Wing blades back, chest raised, beak slightly elevated, Marcy prepared herself. Nodding, she sang.

Time is forever.
It is changed!
EMMANUEL!
The promise from above.
The waiting is ended.
EMMANUEL!
Hope is here.
Hope's name is LOVE.

As Marcy continued, her simple song touched the heart of God. A tear began to flow from the center of God. Marcy noticed it as she glanced at the Holy Presence.

In it seemed reflected all the lights in heaven. She watched it slowly roll and then fall to the earth, like a shooting star. Blazing toward the earth, it collided into the guiding star, which beamed over the stable.

With a breathtaking display of majesty, all the millions and millions of lights caught in that tear were scattered over the snow as far and as ever the eye could see, even the snowlands unknown.

"WOW!" Marcy exclaimed, as she peered over the thumb of God. "It looks like a sea of diamonds. That is so beautiful. Look!" she insisted, as she pointed with her wing to the wondrous display of snow lights.

"That is creative!" she pronounced. Turning toward her heavenly companion, she questioned with knowledge.

"Isn't that one of your names? I mean, I hear men talk about your greatness. Jehovah—creative, isn't it?"

"This is for you and Pud. For remembrance when all the lights of heaven came to earth and stayed!

"As you and Pud humbled your pure hearts to save my promise—my son, so I give this gift of snow lights to mankind to serve as a reminder that heaven came, humbled, to earth and stayed. You are loved! You are loved!"

Stroking her beak with her wing, which Marcy often did when she was putting together an understanding, she thought and rethought, *How wondrous* is *all this.*

Then, the wonder settled in her heart and it was overflowing with joy.

"GLORY TO GOD IN THE HIGHEST, and on earth peace among men with whom He is pleased" (Luke 2: 14).

ALLELUIA! ALLELUIA!

Her heart could not contain the song, just as the night could not contain the blessed birth. The King of Glory had come!

As quick as the twitch of a tail feather, Marcy was next to her friend Pud.

Marcy found herself perched on the edge of the manger, next to a sleeping Pud, who was next to a sleeping babe.

There was a stillness . . . a holy pause in time.

The light still filled the stable. Marcy watched as the shepherds came. Others came. They brought gifts. They brought homage. They prayed and praised before the babe.

Some, Marcy noted, passed by the stable, as if unaware, and disappeared into the cold, dark night.

"Did they not see the light? Did they not sense the joy? Did they not recognize the king of the promise?"

Then her heart and spirit came to a truth. Lowering her head into her feathers, she shuddered as sorrow pierced her peace. *Some men will not recognize Him.*

Marcy tucked that knowledge into her memory of stored truths and bundled it in hope. She felt a nudge.

"Marcy. Marcy. Where have you been?" asked Pud, excited to see her and to share his story of the night.

"Whisper, Pud, The babe is asleep. I must show you something. Come outside."

Pud crawled to the ground and carefully ran to a hole at the back of the stable. Marcy flapped her Wings ever so quietly and flew just above Pud.

As he scampered outside, Pud's round eyes couldn't believe what he saw. His nose sniffed and twittered rapidly, trying to figure out what had happened to the white snow.

Pud slowly placed one paw after another into the snow. He stood motionless for a while. Thinking, staring, sniffing.

"It's snow," he reasoned, delightedly. "Yup. Snow. But it's much prettier now. Tiny lights! What happened, Marcy? A baby is born and the world changes! And, look, Marcy, my, my whiskers! They are straight. My nose is warm."

"Yes, Pud. I see that. Race you to the top of this hill!"

Off the two friends went, making tracks in the newly fallen snow, and each waiting to share a story.

When they reached the top, it was as if somehow the universe lay below and above them. Trying not to be too overwhelmed by the vastness and the events of the night, Marcy and Pud sat silently for a long, friendly time.

They watched with new wonder, the tiny glints of lights, which sparkled across the vast plain. Like Pud and Marcy and the babe, the snow lights were so small, seemingly unnoticeable. Yet these two friends would not know that their one act of good will would be written in snow to light the hearts of men to remembrance forever—a big job!

Through the quiet, Pud asked, "Does God know us, Marcy?"

"By name."

Pud moved closer to Marcy and nestled in the crook of her wing.

"Does God love us, Marcy?"

". . . very, *very* much!."